Winnie-the-Pooh

A Very Grand Thing

Adapted from the stories by A.A. Milne

Halfway between Pooh's house and Piglet's house was a Thoughtful Spot where they met sometimes when they had decided to go and see each other.

Now one autumn morning when the wind had blown all the leaves off the trees in the night, and was trying to blow the branches off, Pooh and Piglet were sitting in the Thoughtful Spot and wondering who to visit.

"Let's go and see *everybody*," said Pooh. "Because when you've been walking in the wind for miles, and you suddenly go into somebody's house, and he says, 'Hallo, Pooh, you're just in time for a little smackerel of something,' and you are, then it's what I call a Friendly Day."

Piglet thought that they ought to have a Reason for going to see everybody, like Looking for Small or Organising an Expotition, if Pooh could think of something.

Pooh could.

"We'll go because it's Thursday," he said, "and we'll go to wish everybody a Very Happy Thursday. Come on, Piglet."

They got up; and when Piglet had sat down again, because he didn't know the wind was so strong, and had been helped up by Pooh, they started off.

They went to Pooh's house first, and luckily Pooh
was at home just as they got there, so he asked them
in, and they had some, and then they went on to
Kanga's house, holding on to each other, and
shouting, "Isn't it?" and "What?" and "I can't hear."
By the time they got to Kanga's house they were so
buffeted that they stayed to lunch. Just at first it
seemed rather cold outside afterwards, so they pushed
on to Rabbit's as quickly as they could.

"We've come to wish you a
Very Happy Thursday," said
Pooh, when he had gone in and
out once or twice just to make
sure that he *could* get out again.

"Why, what's going to happen on Thursday?" asked Rabbit, and when Pooh had explained, and Rabbit, whose life was made up of Important Things, said, "Oh, I thought you'd

really come about something," they sat down for a little…
and by-and-by Pooh and Piglet went on again. The wind was behind them now, so they didn't have to shout.

Christopher Robin was at home by this time, because it was the afternoon, and he was so glad to see them that they stayed there until very nearly tea-time, and then they had a Very Nearly tea, which is one you forget about afterwards, and hurried on to Pooh Corner, so as to see Eeyore before it was too late to have a Proper Tea with Owl.

"Hallo, Eeyore," they called out cheerfully.

"Ah!" said Eeyore. "Lost your way?"

"We just came to see you," said Piglet. "And to see how your house was. Look, Pooh, it's still standing!"

"I know," said Eeyore. "Very odd. Somebody ought to have come down and pushed it over."

"We wondered whether the wind would blow it down," said Pooh.

"Ah, that's why nobody's bothered, I suppose. I thought perhaps they'd forgotten."

Pooh and Piglet shuffled about a little and said, "Well, good-bye, Eeyore," as lingeringly as they could, but they had a long way to go, and wanted to be getting on to Owl's house.

The wind was against them now, and Piglet's ears
streamed behind him like banners as he fought his
way along, and it seemed hours before he got them

into the shelter of the Hundred Acre
Wood and they stood up straight again, to
listen, a little nervously, to the roaring of
the gale among the tree-tops.

"Supposing a tree fell down, Pooh, when we were underneath it?"

"Supposing it didn't," said Pooh after careful thought.

Piglet was comforted by this, and in a little while they were knocking and ringing very cheerfully at Owl's door.

"Hallo, Owl," said Pooh. "I hope we're not too late for – I mean, how are you, Owl? Piglet and I just came to see how you were because it's Thursday."

"Sit down, Pooh, sit down, Piglet," said Owl kindly. "Make yourselves comfortable."

They thanked him, and made themselves as comfortable as they could.

"Because, you see, Owl," said Pooh, "we've been hurrying, so as to be in time for – so as to see you before we went away again."

Owl nodded solemnly.

"Correct me if I am wrong," he said, "but am I right in supposing that it is a very Blusterous day outside?"

"Very," said Piglet, who was quietly thawing his ears, and wishing that he was safely back in his own house.

"I thought so," said Owl. "It was on just such a blusterous day as this that my Uncle Robert, a portrait of whom you see upon the wall on your right, Piglet, while returning in the late forenoon from a – What's that?"

There was a loud cracking noise.

"Look out!" cried Pooh. "Mind the clock! Out of the way, Piglet! Piglet, I'm falling on you!"

"Help!" cried Piglet.

Pooh's side of the room was slowly tilting upwards and his chair began sliding down on Piglet's. The clock slithered gently along the mantel-piece, collecting vases on the way, until they all crashed together on to what had once been the floor, but was now trying to see what it looked like as a wall. Uncle Robert, who was going to be the new hearthrug, and was bringing the rest of his wall with him as carpet, met Piglet's chair just as Piglet was expecting to leave it, and for a little while it became very difficult to remember which was really the north. Then there was another loud crack...

Owl's room collected itself
feverishly … and there was silence.
In a corner of the room, the table-
cloth began to wriggle.

Then it wrapped itself into a ball
and rolled across the room.
Then it jumped up and down once
or twice, and put out two ears.

It rolled across the room again, and unwound itself.

"Pooh," said Piglet nervously.

"Yes?" said one of the chairs.

"Where are we?"

"I'm not quite sure," said the chair.

"Are we – are we in Owl's House?"

"I think so, because we were just going to have tea, and we hadn't had it."

"Oh!" said Piglet. "Well, did Owl *always* have a letter-box in his ceiling?"

"Has he?"

"Yes, look."

"I can't," said Pooh. "I'm face downwards under something, and that, Piglet, is a very bad position for looking at ceilings."

"Well, he has, Pooh."

"Perhaps he's changed it," said Pooh. "Just for a change."

There was a disturbance behind the table in the other corner of the room, and Owl was with them again.

"Ah, Piglet," said Owl, looking very much annoyed; "where's Pooh?"

"I'm not quite sure," said Pooh.

Owl turned at his voice, and frowned at as much of Pooh as he could see.

"Pooh," said Owl severely, "did *you* do that?"

"No," said Pooh humbly. "I don't *think* so."

"Then who did?"

"I think it was the wind," said Piglet. "I think your house has blown down."

"Oh, is that it? I thought it was Pooh."

"No," said Pooh.

"If it was the wind," said Owl, considering the matter, "then it wasn't Pooh's fault. No blame can be attached to him."

With these kind words Owl and Piglet pushed and pulled at the arm-chair, and in a little while Pooh came out from underneath, and was able to look round him again.

"Well!" said Owl. "This is a nice state of things! What are we going to do, Pooh?"

"Can you think of anything?" asked Piglet.

"Because," said Owl, "we can't go out by what used to be the front door. Something's fallen on it."

"But how else *can* you go out?" asked Piglet anxiously.

"That is the Problem, Piglet, to which I am asking Pooh to give his mind."

Pooh sat on the floor which had once been a wall, and gazed up at the ceiling which had once been another wall, with a front door in it which had once been a front door, and tried to give his mind to it.

"Could you fly up to the letter-box with Piglet on your back?" he asked.

"No," said Piglet quickly. "He couldn't."

"Because you see, Owl, if we could get Piglet into the letter-box, he might squeeze through the place where the letters come, and climb down the tree and run for help."

Owl explained that he didn't have the Necessary Dorsal Muscles, and Piglet said, "Then we'd better think of something else," and began to at once.

But Pooh's mind had gone back to the day when he had saved Piglet from the flood, and everybody had admired him so much; and as that didn't often happen, he thought he would like it to happen again. And suddenly, just as it had come before, an idea came to him.

"Owl," said Pooh. "I have thought of something."

"Astute and Helpful Bear," said Owl.

Pooh looked proud at being called a stout and helpful bear, and said modestly that he just happened to think of it. You tied a piece of string to Piglet, and you flew up to the letter-box, with the other end in your beak, and you pushed it through the wire and brought it down to the floor, and you and Pooh pulled hard at this end, and Piglet went slowly up at the other end. And there you were.

"And there Piglet is," said Owl. "If the string doesn't break."

"Supposing it does?" asked Piglet, really wanting to know.

"It won't break," whispered Pooh comfortingly, "because you're a Small Animal, and I'll stand underneath, and if you save us all, it will be a Very Grand Thing to talk about afterwards."

Piglet felt much better after this, and when everything was ready, and he found himself slowly going up to the ceiling, he was so proud that he would have called out "Look at me!" if he hadn't been afraid that Pooh and Owl would let go of their end of the string and look at him.

"Up we go!" said Pooh cheerfully.

"The ascent is proceeding as expected," said Owl helpfully. Soon it was over. Piglet opened the letter-box, climbed in and squeezed out to the other side.

Happy and excited he turned round to squeak a last message to
the prisoners.

"It's all right," he called through the letter-box. "Your tree is
blown right over, Owl, and there's a branch across the door, but
Christopher Robin and I will be back in about half an hour.
Good-bye, Pooh!" And without waiting to hear Pooh's
answering "Good-bye, and thank you, Piglet," he was off.

"Half an hour," said Owl, settling himself comfortably. "That
will just give me time to finish that story I was telling you about
my Uncle Robert – a portrait of whom you see underneath you.
Now let me see, where was I? Oh, yes. It was on just such a
blusterous day as this that my Uncle Robert —"

Pooh closed his eyes.